Keep Walking!

In Honor of Kamil Patel

"You Never Walk Alone"

www.mascotbooks.com

Keep Walking

For more information, please contact:
Mascot Books
620 Herndon Parkway #320
Herndon, VA 20170
info@mascotbooks.com

Library of Congress Control Number: 2018914053

CPSIA Code: PRTWP0119A
ISBN-13: 978-1-64307-424-5

Printed in Malaysia

Keep Walking

Written by **W. S. Mason**

Illustrated by **Maima Widya Adiputri**

When your tiny hands are tumbling,
When you aren't quite yet talking,

Even if you're stumbling,
Please, my love, keep walking.

When rain is pouring down on you,

And dark clouds follow you around,

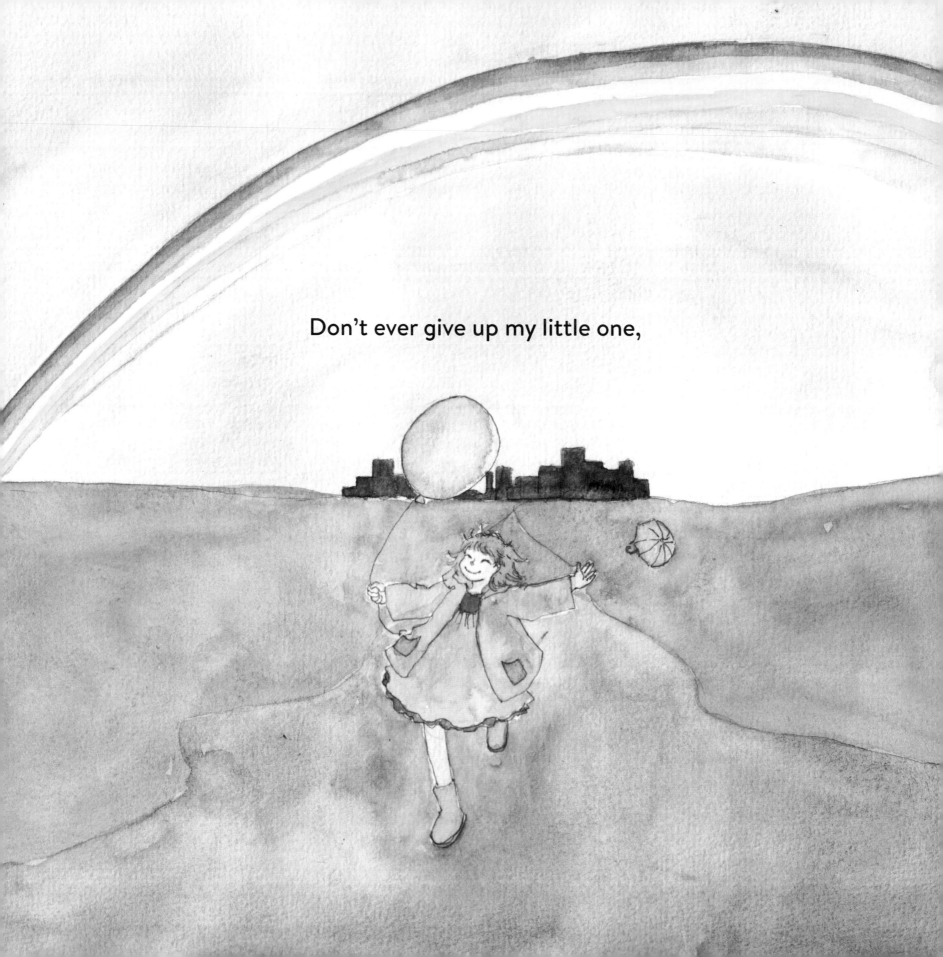

Don't ever give up my little one,

Keep walking – you'll soon be found.

When you enter into school,
And you're asked to write by chalking,

Know that you'll feel better soon,
Keep walking – even just a tad.

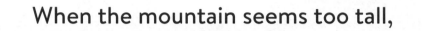

When the mountain seems too tall,

Or the river seems too rough,

Trust the voice inside your heart,

Keep walking – even when you've had enough.

When others hurt your feelings,
And blue skies are nowhere near,

Always know the sun shines again,
Keep walking – the sky will soon be clear.

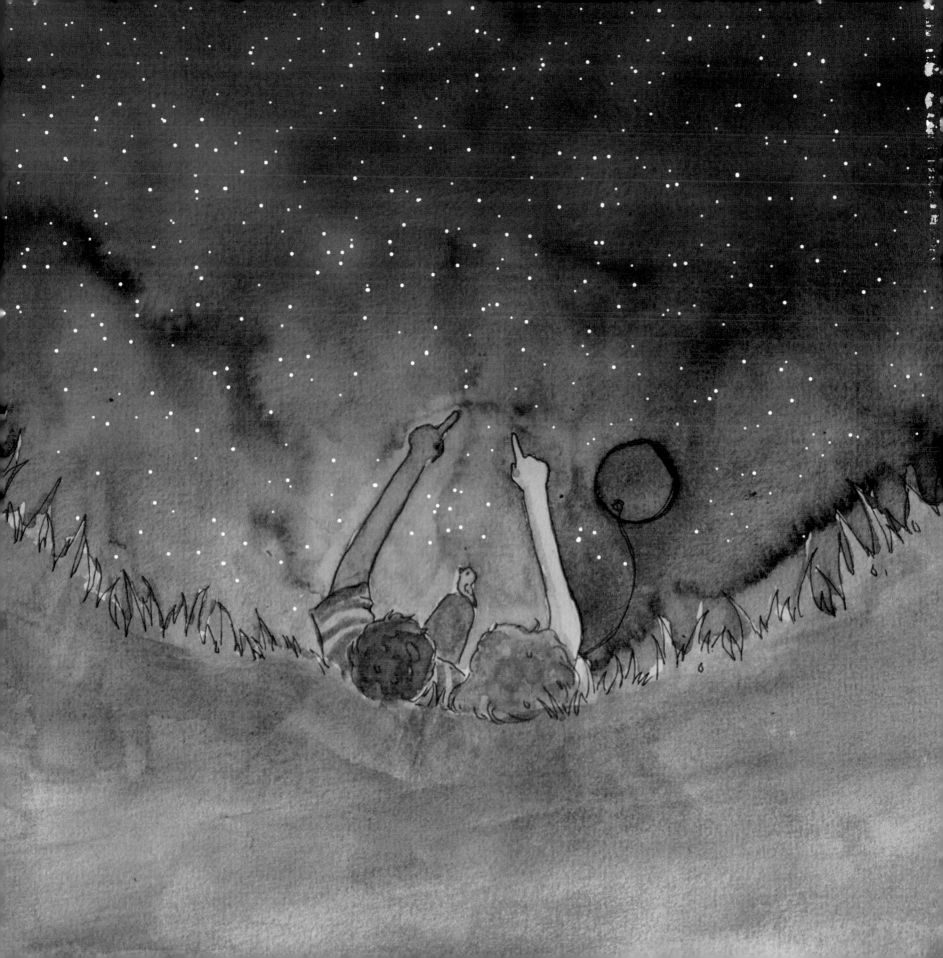

When friends and family leave us,
And the pain of change is stalking,

Trust that it will be okay,
My darling, please keep walking.

When you're grown and on your own,
And if it's more than you can take,

Remember dear, you'll be okay,
Just keep walking – you will not break.

As your own children learn to walk,

And they begin to explore,

Try not to feel so lonely, love,

You've walked this far...

And you can walk some more.

When your knees are weak and brittle,

And the sleepiness is hawking,

Remember to follow the light my love,

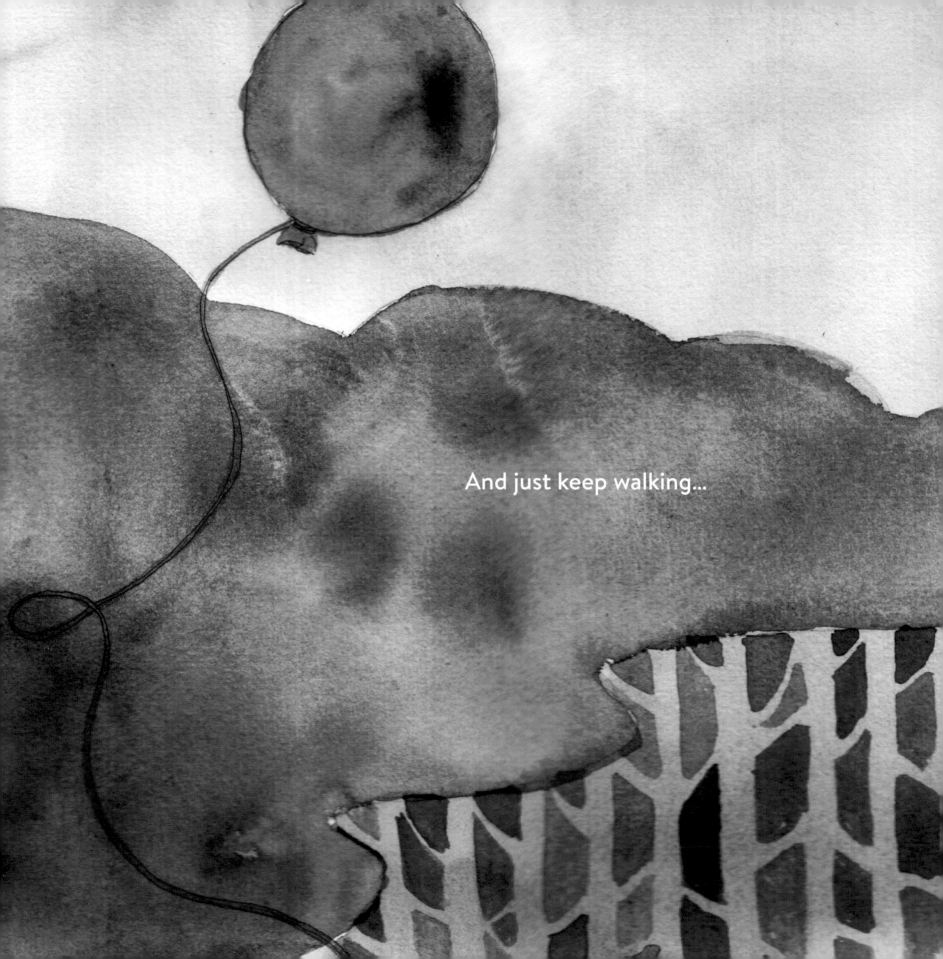

And just keep walking...